To my children, Isabella, James, Anthony, Joseph and Gabrielle.
Look to the heavens and become all that you can be.

—J. D. O.

To my granddaughter, Charlotte Alivia Pearl.
I cherish our morning walks, which happen most every day.
And soon, like going to outer space, she'll be up, up and away.

—G. G. R.

ENDEAVOUR'S LONG JOURNEY

Celebrating 19 Years of Space Exploration

Written by **John D. Olivas**

Illustrated by **Gayle Garner Roski**

East West Discovery Press

Manhattan Beach, CA

FOREWORD

When I was seven years old, my father took me to the Hayden Planetarium in New York City. I saw telescopes, pictures of the planets, images of the stars in the heavens, and actual meteorites that had fallen to earth. It was fascinating, and on the ride back home I told my father I wanted to become an engineer and design rocket ships that would someday take astronauts to space. Recognizing my interest in science, space, and the quest for knowledge, my father took me to the library and introduced me to a wide variety of books. After school I would read as many books as time would allow to learn about science, great people, and how to build things like model planes that I could actually fly. Those studies grew and continued even as an adult. Eventually I graduated from college and accepted a job at National Aeronautics and Space Administration (NASA). After many years of designing and managing spacecraft projects at NASA and later at a private corporation, the President of the United States asked me to become the director of America's Space Program as the Administrator of NASA. It was a dream come true for me, which started with my father taking me on a trip to a museum and exposing me to good books.

Books like *Endeavour's Long Journey* are important to inspire young people like you to think about mathematics, science, and technology in a fun way. It may lead to a fantastic career like I have had, whether becoming an engineer, an astronaut, or even the director of NASA. This story demonstrates how a very diverse group of hard-working people worked together to accomplish important and difficult tasks. We should all strive to make a difference as individuals. And as we do, we can help change the world for the better.

Daniel Saul Goldin
9th Administrator of NASA
April 1, 1992 – May 21, 2001

INTRODUCTORY STATEMENT

Growing up as an African American in Columbia, South Carolina, in the segregated South, I never dreamed of becoming a pilot and especially not an astronaut. My mom and dad were both schoolteachers and they always told me that I could do anything I wanted if I studied hard, dreamed big, and never let anyone tell me what I could and couldn't do. With the encouragement and support of my parents, I studied very hard to get into the United States Naval Academy and graduated to become a United States Marine Corps Officer and pilot—later a Naval Test Pilot. But in spite of their urging to reach for the stars with my dreams, it was not until I met and talked with the late Dr. Ron McNair, also an African American from South Carolina and a member of the first group of NASA astronauts selected in 1978 to fly the Space Shuttle, that I decided to apply for the Shuttle Program. Ron told me much the same as Jojo is told by *Endeavour* in the book: "Dream your dreams, and make them happen." With Ron's mentorship, I did become an astronaut and flew the Shuttle four times into space, commanding two of my missions. Being part of the Space Shuttle Program was an exciting and rewarding part of my 34-year Marine Corps career. The Shuttle Program brought critical diversity to the human spaceflight program, as from that first class in 1978 to today, it has included people from many races, cultures, nations, and religions as well as very diverse technical backgrounds. Young boys and girls everywhere are inspired by information on space flight and the orbital vehicles that were part of the Space Shuttle Program's phenomenal 30-year era.

Charles F. Bolden Jr.
12th Administrator of NASA

"We're going to the science center!" I scream with excitement.

We have been there before, but my sister, Bella, was very little then. I remember pretending to be a pilot in the cool planes they have out front.

Mom tells us, "Today is going to be extra special. Do you remember seeing the space shuttle *Endeavour* flying across the country on the back of another aircraft on the television? We're going to see her close up."

As we arrive, hundreds of people walk toward the museum. We see *Endeavour*. The black and white space shuttle is huge! Everyone is "oohing" and "ahhing."

"She and the other shuttles were a very important part of human exploration in space. She has journeyed a long, long way," Mom explains.

Endeavour Replica
Ratio 1:8

"Mom, why do you keep calling *Endeavour* a 'she'?" I ask.

"Well Jojo, it's simple. Just like I take care of you and your sister, *Endeavour* took care of all the astronauts who flew her. The astronauts think of *Endeavour* kind of like their mother. They really do. And the astronauts treat her with great care and also respect, as they depend on her."

I think about how this enormous shuttle has carried astronauts, and I wonder what it would have been like to be part of the crew—to eat, sleep, and work inside.

Suddenly, I feel myself floating...

Then, a soft voice whispers, "Thanks for your visit, Jojo."

What is that? I ask myself.

"It's me, *Endeavour*!" Her voice is kind and gentle, but firm—like Mom's. "Come join me on the journey I have traveled."

I look at my clothes—now a blue flight suit, the kind astronauts wear! Then the world begins to fade.

All that is left is *Endeavour* and me. It is pitch black with millions of stars, and Earth is far below. But I'm not afraid. Floating in space is fun! Now I know what it feels like to be in microgravity.

Gravity

The further away from Earth you are, the less and less pull there is of the Earth's gravity. To feel almost no gravity, you would have to be almost to the Moon over 200,000 miles away. However, the shuttle never travels that far from the planet, only about 300 miles up. The gravity that high up is actually still very close to here on Earth. Astronauts float for a different reason. In order to avoid falling back to Earth, the shuttle goes around the Earth very fast. Like going fast on a playground merry-go-round, you are pulled away from the center.

The shuttle is going about 17,500 miles an hour around Earth. Even though the shuttle is being pulled back toward Earth by gravity, it is traveling so fast and so high, it is actually falling around the Earth. This is known as microgravity. Since the shuttle and astronauts are actually falling around the Earth, they float together in orbit. When the shuttle is ready to come home, it just slows down and falls back to Earth.

Next, I find myself inside *Endeavour,* on the flight deck. I look at the instrument panel, which shows we are traveling at 17,500 miles per hour! "That's how fast we need to travel to stay in orbit," she says.

"Wow!" I am amazed.

"But getting into space is just the start. This is my first mission," *Endeavour* explains. I watch the astronauts on the mid-deck, frantically preparing for an urgent situation. A satellite that has been launched into space is not working properly. The astronauts need to perform a spacewalk to grab the satellite and bring it back to Earth.

"It is a dangerous mission. This is the very first and only time that three spacewalkers left the ship at the same time. They actually captured the satellite with their hands."

"The air lock in the mid-deck allowed the astronauts to leave their comfy crew compartment for the potential danger outside. They use a very special spacesuit to do this," she adds.

"In space, the temperature can reach 200 degrees Fahrenheit in the sun and minus 200 degrees Fahrenheit in the shade. The suits also help the astronauts breathe. There is no air in space, so if anything happens to the suits, the astronauts are in big trouble!"

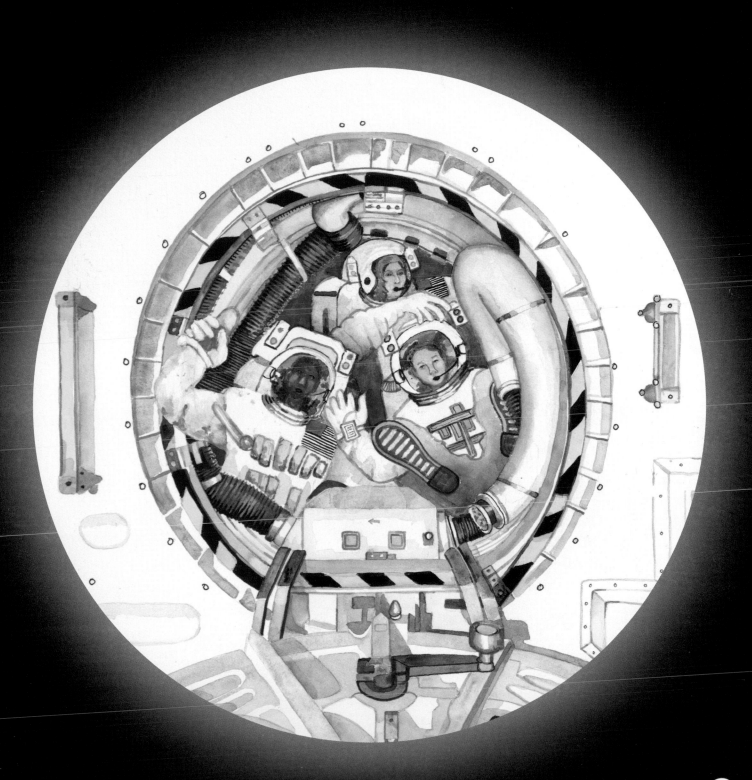

As the spacewalker struggles with the satellite, one astronaut seems to be in trouble. He twitches his face and scrunches his nose. He moans.

"What's wrong?" Ground Control asks anxiously. The astronaut moans again, and everyone waits for his answer.

"My nose is itchy, and I can't scratch it through the helmet!" We all breathe a sigh of relief. Then the voice crackles over the radio again. "Houston, we have the satellite," Ground Control announces. "The mission is a success."

"Were you built just to rescue satellites?" I ask *Endeavour*.

"Oh, much more than that," she says. "I was built to replace the shuttle *Challenger*, who had an accident."

"We learned in school that one of the space shuttles actually blew up after it was launched. Was that *Challenger*?"

"Yes," says *Endeavour*. "After a small seal broke on one of the rockets during her launch, she never made it back home. The break caused the rocket to explode. Seven brave astronauts died on that mission. One of them was the very first teacher to go into space, Christie McAuliffe. She taught high school before she was trained to become an astronaut."

Endeavour explains in a brave voice, "The men and women who built *Challenger* were determined not to give up. With everyone's support behind them, they built me. I soared into space on my first mission in 1992."

"It must have been sad for everyone after what happened to your sister, but I'm glad that you were built. Watching the satellite rescue is awesome." I smile.

As I float through the mid-deck, I see scientists busy working on various experiments

"I'd like you to meet my special team," *Endeavour* says.

"This young lady is Dr. Mae Jemison. I brought her into space, making her the first female African American astronaut. These young men are Dr. Mamoru Mohri, the first Japanese astronaut in the shuttle program, and John Herrington, the first Native American astronaut to walk in space."

"I didn't know astronauts were doctors," I exclaim.

"Astronauts come from all walks of life. During my journeys, I brought doctors, engineers, pilots, astronomers, geologists, and many other types of astronauts into space," she explains.

"Aren't all astronauts the same?" I ask.

"No, Jojo. Astronauts with different types of training and backgrounds work together as a team to complete many different types of projects."

This is getting more interesting. "Tell me about your other missions," I add.

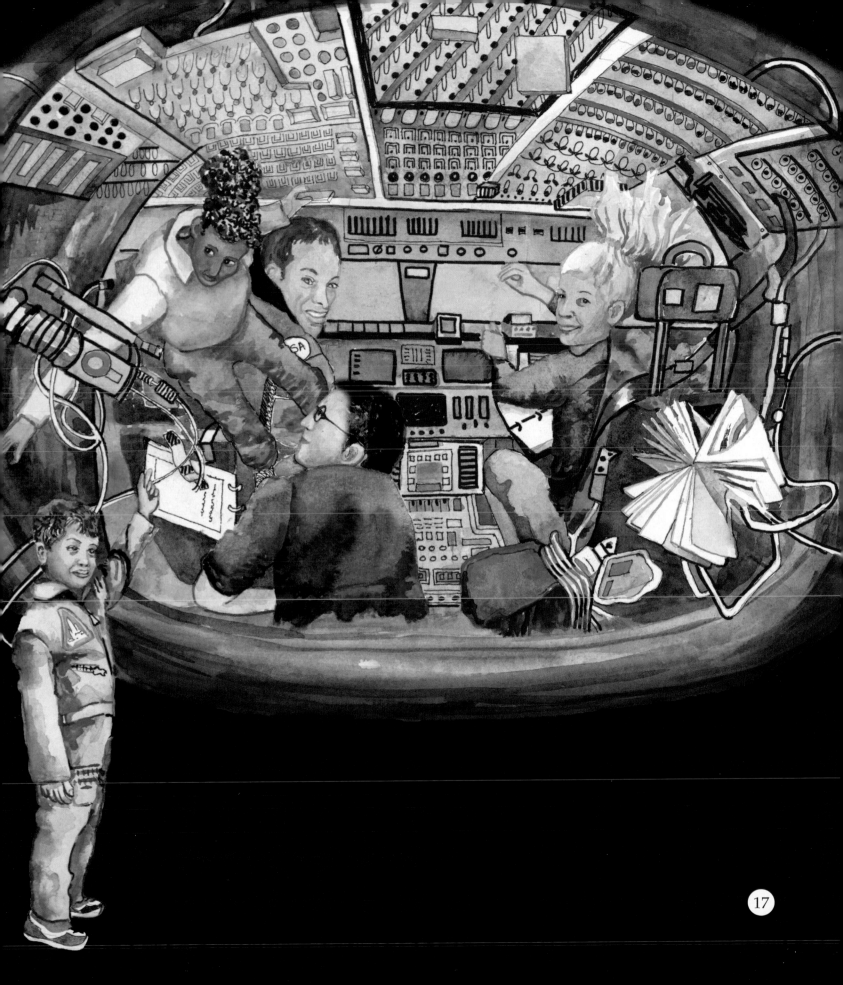

How can the Hubble Space Telescope see into the past?

It can take a long time for the light from stars to get to us. The sunlight we see every day takes about eight minutes to get here. So we see how the sun looked eight minutes before. Hubble can get clear images billions of miles into space. When we see some distant stars, we see how they looked millions of years ago. Observing the most distant stars and galaxies, we can look far back in time, close to when the universe was formed. The universe is about 13.75 billion years old. How old is that? Well, modern humans have only been on Earth 200,000 years, which means that much of the light we see in the night sky actually left their stars well before humans ever even existed on our planet.

"In 1993, one of my most daring missions was to perform the very first eye operation in space," *Endeavour* says.

"Really! Who did you operate on?"

"It was an operation on the Hubble Space Telescope," she tells me. "It was a one-of-a-kind surgery to help Hubble see images deep into space, millions of miles away.

"What was wrong with the telescope?" I ask.

"Look outside my windows, and you'll see for yourself," *Endeavour* says. I watch as the astronauts catch the big telescope with the 50-foot robot arm and pull it into the shuttle's open payload bay.

"A few years earlier, the telescope was successfully launched into orbit, but its view became fuzzy because one of its mirrors was out of shape. So I brought a crew of astronauts to perform the very difficult task of fixing the fuzziness by putting 'glasses' on Hubble and adding new instruments," *Endeavour* explains.

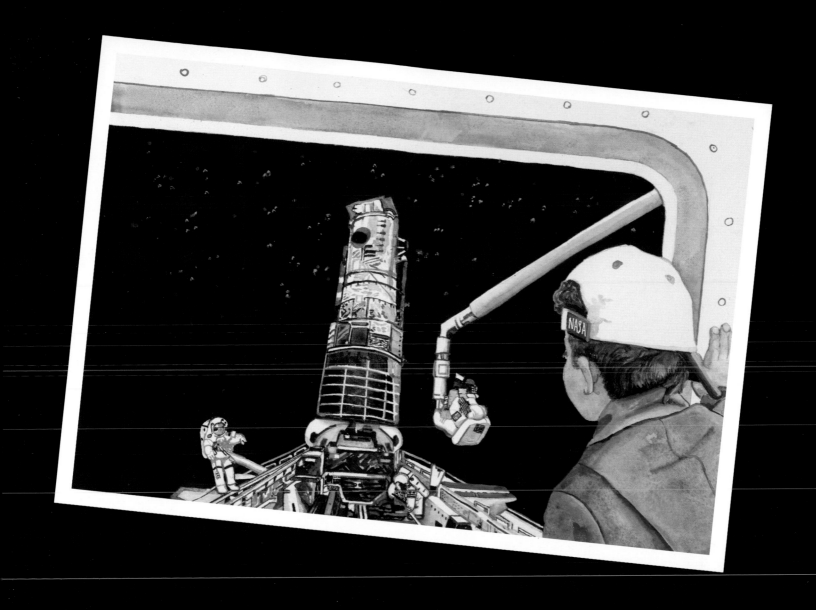

The astronauts move so gently around the telescope in their bulky spacesuits. The crew inside are focusing on their jobs, as are the spacewalkers. I can hear the concerned voices of the controllers back on Earth. The whole team works to fix the fragile telescope. Everything has to be done perfectly.

At last, the words the crew are waiting for comes from Mission Control. "Great news, *Endeavour*! Your mission is complete. Hubble can see!" All the astronauts aboard *Endeavour* smile and hug each other in congratulations. The Hubble can now take the best pictures of the stars and galaxies ever taken. And the pictures are amazing.

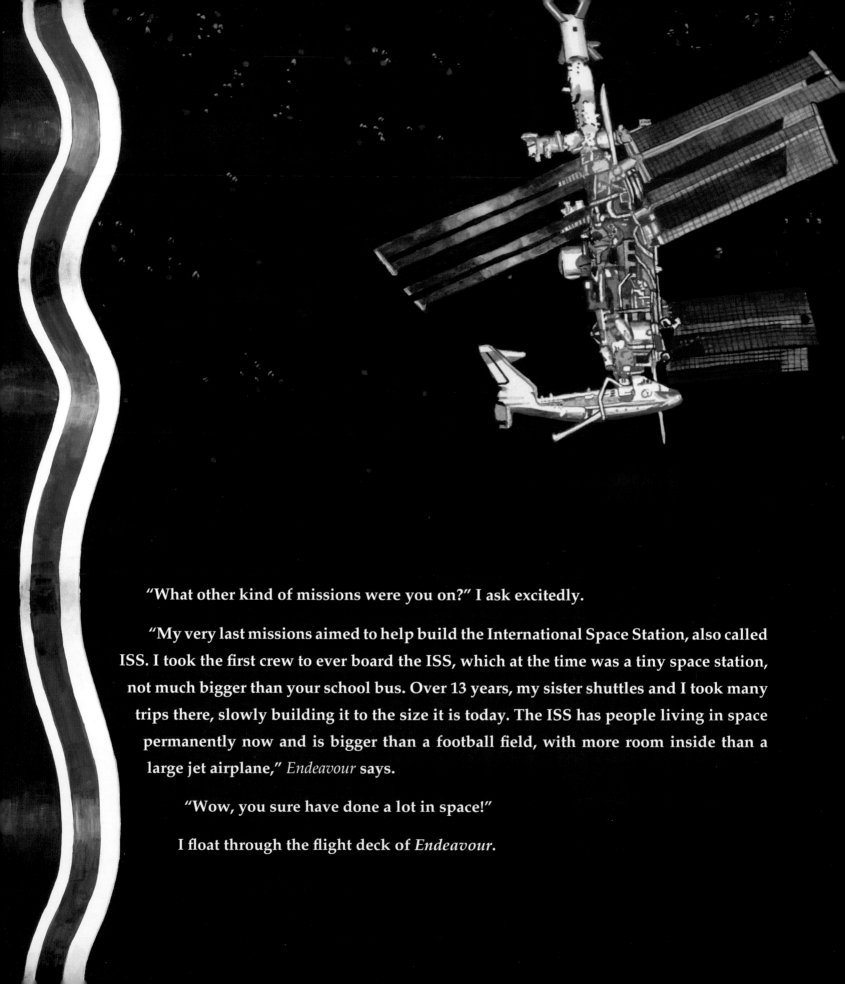

"What other kind of missions were you on?" I ask excitedly.

"My very last missions aimed to help build the International Space Station, also called ISS. I took the first crew to ever board the ISS, which at the time was a tiny space station, not much bigger than your school bus. Over 13 years, my sister shuttles and I took many trips there, slowly building it to the size it is today. The ISS has people living in space permanently now and is bigger than a football field, with more room inside than a large jet airplane," *Endeavour* says.

"Wow, you sure have done a lot in space!"

I float through the flight deck of *Endeavour*.

"On June 1, 2011, I completed my last mission, journeying to the ISS one final time with an experiment to help scientists understand the beginnings of our universe," she explains. "You see, Jojo, my very long journey was not one that I took alone. Together with astronauts, scientists, engineers, and technicians, we explore space as a team of humans and the machines they made. In fact, it wouldn't surprise me if you know one of them."

Endeavour smiles mischievously.

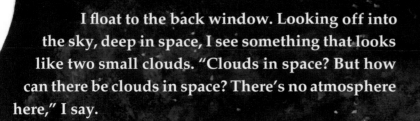

I float to the back window. Looking off into the sky, deep in space, I see something that looks like two small clouds. "Clouds in space? But how can there be clouds in space? There's no atmosphere here," I say.

"You are right. There are no clouds in space. Look deeper Jojo. What do you see?" she whispers back.

I look again and strain my eyes. Deeper and deeper I look. "Those are not clouds! They are filled with stars!"

"That's right. What you see are galaxies, a group of millions of stars. They are called 'The Magellanic Clouds'—our two neighboring galaxies that are visible from Earth," she explains.

Distance to the Stars

The Sun is about 93 million miles away from Earth. The next nearest stars are Alpha Centauri. They are much further, trillions of miles away. So we measure the distance to stars in terms of light-years which is how far light travels in one year. Light travels about 6 trillion miles in one year. Alpha Centauri are more than four light-years away. That basically means that the light leaving Alpha Centauri we see today left it over four years ago. The farthest stars we have seen are billions of light-years away.

Millions and millions of stars, all clustered together to make what looks like the two hazy clouds. Here I am inside *Endeavour*, in my own Milky Way galaxy, looking at stars, far, far away. My mind begins to wonder: *Does that galaxy have a planet like Earth? Is there life there?* I wonder if something is there now, looking back at me, asking the same question.

"This is what's so special about space. For 19 years I flew, looking at sights like this. After so many years of exploring, there are still many questions left unanswered," she says with pride.

As Endeavour continues to tell about the many questions she still has about the universe, I begin to float away from her. We drift further and further apart as I begin to fall back to Earth.

Then I hear that very familiar voice.

"JoJo," Endeavour whispers, "I've been on a long journey, and I'm happy I've been able to share my wonderful experience with you. I'm ready for a well-deserved rest. Go tell your friends to come visit me. I'll be here ready to take them on my incredible journey."

I am sad. I don't want the adventure to end. I want to fly with Endeavour and continue the exploration of space.

"Remember, I was built by people who believe that humans should explore space. Now it's your turn to dream and build the next ship to carry you and the next generation of astronauts to the great beyond.

"Dream your dreams, and make them happen. Explore all the secrets the universe has to share," she says as her voice becomes fainter…and then fades away.

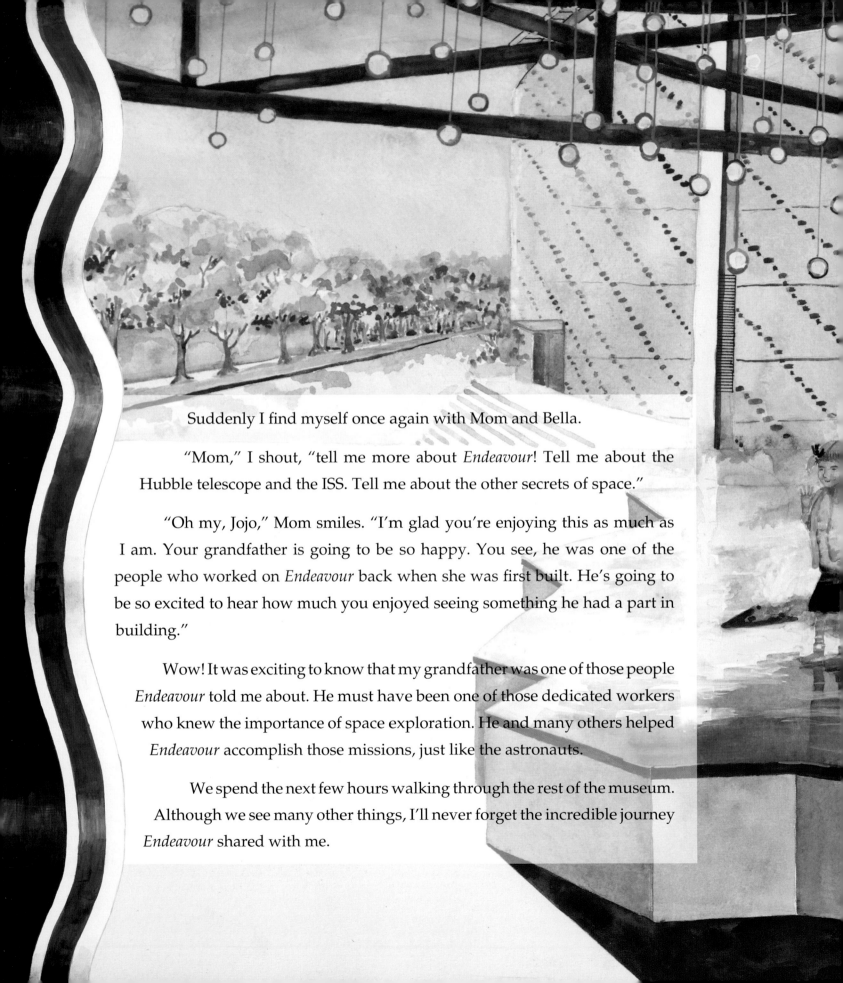

Suddenly I find myself once again with Mom and Bella.

"Mom," I shout, "tell me more about *Endeavour*! Tell me about the Hubble telescope and the ISS. Tell me about the other secrets of space."

"Oh my, Jojo," Mom smiles. "I'm glad you're enjoying this as much as I am. Your grandfather is going to be so happy. You see, he was one of the people who worked on *Endeavour* back when she was first built. He's going to be so excited to hear how much you enjoyed seeing something he had a part in building."

Wow! It was exciting to know that my grandfather was one of those people *Endeavour* told me about. He must have been one of those dedicated workers who knew the importance of space exploration. He and many others helped *Endeavour* accomplish those missions, just like the astronauts.

We spend the next few hours walking through the rest of the museum. Although we see many other things, I'll never forget the incredible journey *Endeavour* shared with me.

MEET *ENDEAVOUR*

Endeavour was the fifth shuttle built by the United States. It resides at the California Science Center in California. Her sisters *Atlantis* and *Discovery* presently reside at the Kennedy Space Center Visitor Complex in Florida and the Smithsonian's National Air and Space Museum in Washington DC, respectively. The very first orbiter, *Enterprise,* is at the Intrepid Sea, Air, and Space Museum in New York. Together with *Atlantis, Challenger, Columbia,* and *Discovery,* the shuttle fleet took astronauts from all over the world into space. They proved that humans could live and work in space. Together, they built a permanent colony in space, the International Space Station. Even today, astronauts live and work in a place that could have never existed had it not been for the men and women who comprised the space shuttle program.

ENDEAVOUR FUN FACTS

1

Named after an 18th-century ship led by Captain James Cook of Britain. The first and only shuttle named by elementary and secondary school students in a naming contest.

3

To reach its home at the California Science Center, *Endeavour* was towed for two days at two mph through crowded Los Angeles streets, requiring the removal of power lines, traffic lights, and over 400 trees.

2

During *Endeavour*'s 25 missions, she traveled 123 million miles. That's about the same as 260 round trips from the Earth to the Moon.

4 *Endeavour* was the youngest space shuttle. Her 19 years of flight missions ran from 1992 until she was retired in 2011.

5 The payload bay of *Endeavour* is big enough to carry cargo about the size of a school bus into and back from space.

6 *Endeavour* completed *Challenger*'s mission of taking a teacher into space. In 2007, she carried Barbara Morgan, an Idaho schoolteacher. Ms. Morgan eventually became an astronaut.

7 The hottest part of the space shuttle journey was during entry back into Earth's atmosphere—not launch! Returning home heated up the wings to about 3,000 degrees Fahrenheit or 1,650 degrees Celsius.

8 Two minutes after liftoff, when the rocket boosters fell away, the shuttle and external fuel tank were traveling at more than 3,000 miles per hour.

13 The waste generated by the fuel cells on *Endeavour* provided drinking water for the astronauts. These fuel cells also provided all electric power to the spacecraft.

9 *Endeavour* is 122 feet long and 57 feet high, with a wingspan of 78 feet.

10 *Endeavour* was built from parts that remained from building *Discovery* and *Atlantis*.

11 The external fuel tank used on *Endeavour*'s last mission was damaged and repaired after being struck by Hurricane Katrina.

12 When fully loaded, *Endeavour* could carry as much as 54,000 pounds into space. That's about the same as carrying five full-grown elephants!

ENDEAVOUR'S FAMOUS FIRSTS

(Flight mission: 1992 – 2011)

MISSION POSSIBLE

Performed the first spacewalk involving three astronauts and four spacewalks—a risky maneuver!

Endeavour crewmembers of mission STS-49 hold onto a 4.5 ton satellite.

BREAKING BOUNDARIES

Carried the first African American female astronaut, Mae Jemison, into space; the first Japanese astronaut, Mamoru Mohri, in the shuttle program; and the first Native American astronaut John Bennett Herrington of the Chickasaw Nation to walk in space.

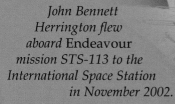

John Bennett Herrington flew aboard Endeavour mission STS-113 to the International Space Station in November 2002.

VISION QUEST

Completed the first service mission to the Hubble Space Telescope in 1993.

Astronaut F. Story Musgrave, anchored on the end of a robot arm, prepares to be lifted to the top of the Hubble Space Telescope for repair work.

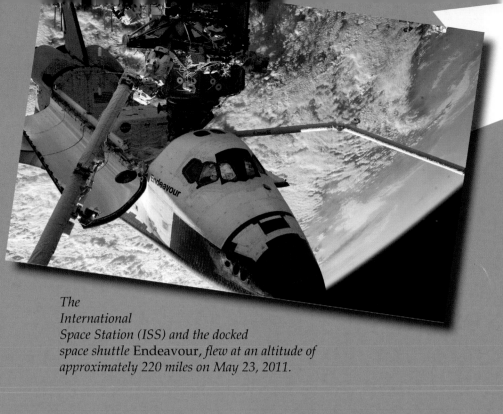

The International Space Station (ISS) and the docked space shuttle Endeavour, *flew at an altitude of approximately 220 miles on May 23, 2011.*

Endeavour *docked to the ISS on her final mission in 2011.*

CHUTING A LANDING

Became the first space shuttle to use the parachute, known as a drag chute, during a shuttle landing.

PROMOTING UNITY

Assembled the Unity Module, the first U.S. component of the International Space Station

Endeavour *touched down with a drag chute at Edwards Air Force Base on Nov. 30, 2008 on the base's Runway 4.*

Discovery's Famous Firsts

(Flight mission: 1984 – 2011)

- Holds the record of 39 flight missions, more than any other space shuttle or any spacecraft.

- Became the only shuttle ever to fly one of the original seven Mercury astronauts. John Glenn first flew in space in 1962, and then flew his second mission on *Discovery* in 1998—36 years later! John Glenn was not only the first American to orbit the Earth, he was also the oldest astronaut to fly in space at the age of 77.

- Carried Eileen Collins, the first American female astronaut to pilot *Discovery*, and Bernard Harris, the first African American to walk in space aboard *Discovery* on the STS-63 mission in 1995. It linked up in orbit with Russia's Mir space station.

- Carried the first Russian cosmonaut, Sergei Krikalev, to launch in an American spacecraft, in 1994.

- Carried Ellen Ochoa, the first female Hispanic American to fly in space, aboard STS-56 in 1993.

- Deployed the Hubble Space Telescope in 1990.

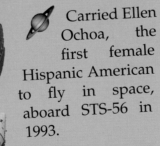

Atlantis's Famous Firsts

(Flight mission: 1985 – 2011)

- Carried Rodolfo Neri Vela, the first Mexican in space, in 1985 on STS-61B.

- Carried Claude Nicollier, the first Swiss citizen to fly in space, aboard STS-46 in 1992.

- Became the first shuttle to dock with a space station, Mir, on STS-71 in 1995. It was also the 100th U.S.-manned space flight.

- Performed the final Hubble Space Telescope Servicing Mission 4 on STS-125 in 2009.

- Performed the final mission for the space shuttle program on STS-135 in 2011.

COLUMBIA'S FAMOUS FIRSTS

(Flight mission: 1981 – 2003)

- Became the very first space shuttle to fly in space.

- Completed the longest shuttle mission on STS-80 for a total of 17 days, 15 hours, and 53 minutes.

- Flew the smallest crew of astronauts, of two, on the very first shuttle mission of the space shuttle program.

- Became the first manned spacecraft to be reused, on November 12, 1981.

- Became the first spacecraft to carry a crew of six people into space and also flew the first Spacelab module in 1983.

- Carried Franklin Chang Diaz, the first Hispanic American in space, in 1986; the first Vietnamese American, Eugene Huu Chau, in 1992; and the first American female of Indian descent, Kalpana Chawla, in 1997.

- Became the only space shuttle to be destroyed during re-entry. On February 1, 2003, returning home, it disintegrated with all its crew members.

The Columbia crew lost during STS-107 mission in 2003. Front row from left: astronauts Rick D. Husband, mission commander, and William C. McCool, pilot. Standing: astronauts David M. Brown, Laurel B. Clark, Kalpana Chawla and Michael P. Anderson, all mission specialists; and Ilan Ramon, payload specialist representing the Israeli Space Agency.

CHALLENGER'S FAMOUS FIRSTS

(Flight mission: 1983 – 1986)

- Performed the first spacewalk during a space shuttle mission on April 4, 1983.

- Carried Dr. Sally Ride, the first American woman in space, in 1983. She was a mission specialist on STS-7.

- Carried Guion Stewart Bluford, the first African American in space, aboard STS-8 in 1983.

- Carried Kathryn D. Sullivan, the first American woman to make a spacewalk, in 1984. STS-41-G was the first mission to carry two women on the same mission, and also to carry Marc Garneau, the first Canadian in space.

- Carried Taylor Gun Jin Wangin, the first ethnic Chinese person to go into space, in 1985.

- Lost seven crew members on the morning of Jan. 28, 1986, when a booster engine failed, causing the *Challenger* to break apart just 73 seconds after launch.

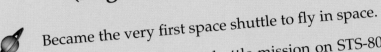

The lost Challenger crew of STS-51-L: Front row from left: Mike Smith, Dick Scobee, Ron McNair. Back row: Ellison Onizuka, Christa McAuliffe, Greg Jarvis, Judith Resnik.

SPACE QUIZ

1. Who was the first American astronaut to fly in space?

    a. Alan Shepard
    b. John Glenn
    c. Neil Armstrong
    d. Edwin Aldrin

2. Who was the first Hispanic American astronaut to fly in space?

    a. Fernando Caldeiro
    b. Franklin Chang-Diaz
    c. Ellen Ochoa
    d. John "Danny" Olivas

3. What is the main exhaust of the space shuttle launch?

    a. hydrogen
    b. carbon dioxide
    c. oxygen
    d. water.

4. Which country invented the first rockets?

    a. Soviet Union
    b. United States
    c. China
    d. Germany

5. How many parts of a space shuttle were ever made up of?

    a. 1 million
    b. 2.5 million
    c. 5.5 million
    d. 7 million

6. How long does it take during liftoff for a space shuttle go from 0 mph to over 17,000 mph?

    a. 8 ½ minutes
    b. 12 minutes
    c. 20 minutes
    d. 35 minutes

7. How much does an entire space shuttle with its tank and solid rocket motors weigh?

    a. 2 million lbs.
    b. 6 million lbs.
    c. 8 million lbs.
    d. 10 million lbs.

8. Who was the only sitting U.S. President to personally see a spacecraft launch?

    a. President Bill Clinton
    b. President John Kennedy
    c. President Ronald Regan
    d. President Barack Obama

9. How long is a space shuttle?

    a. Three school buses long
    b. Five school buses long
    c. Seven school buses long
    d. Eight school buses long

10. Which was the only space shuttle never to fly in space?

    a. *Atlantis*
    b. *Challenger*
    c. *Columbia*
    d. *Enterprise*

Please see answers on page 36.

Endeavour's Final Journey to the California Science Center

The skyline of downtown Los Angeles pierces the mid-day haze above space shuttle *Endeavour* and its modified 747 Shuttle Carrier Aircraft during its flyover of Los Angeles landmarks near the conclusion of its Tour of California on its final ferry flight, Sept. 21, 2012.

Thousands of spectators gathered in front of the Forum in Inglewood, California, as *Endeavour* stopped temporarily for a celebration as it headed overland to its new home at the California Science Center in Los Angeles on Saturday, Oct. 13, 2012.

Endeavour is on display at the Samuel Oschin Space Shuttle *Endeavour* Display Pavilion at the California Science Center. *Endeavour's* ultimate mission is to inspire future generations of explorers and scientists.

Text copyright © 2013 by East West Discovery Press
Illustrations copyright © 2013 by Gayle Garner Roski
Introductory Statement by Charles F. Bolden Jr. is a Work of the U.S. Government.

Published by:
East West Discovery Press
P.O. Box 3585, Manhattan Beach, CA 90266
Phone: 310-545-3730, Fax: 310-545-3731
Website: www.eastwestdiscovery.com

Written by John D. Olivas
Illustrated by Gayle Garner Roski
Edited by Icy Smith and Michael Smith
Design and production by Jennifer Thomas and Icy Smith
Photo research by Icy Smith
Photo credits: p. 28, *Endeavour* being towed down the street by Jennifer Thomas; p. 35, Endeavour exhibit display by Michael Smith; all other photos courtesy of NASA.

Library of Congress Cataloging-in-Publication Data

Olivas, John D.
   Endeavour's long journey : celebrating 19 years of space exploration / written by John D. Olivas ; illustrated by Gayle Garner Roski ; [photos, NASA].
      p. cm.
Summary: While visiting the science museum with his mother and sister, Jojo finds himself on a journey through space as the retired space shuttle Endeavour describes her missions and the people involved.Includes "fun facts" about Endeavour, "famous firsts" of five space shuttles, quizzes, and a glossary.
   Includes bibliographical references and index.
   ISBN 978-0-9856237-2-2 (hardcover : alk. paper) [1. Endeavour (Space shuttle)--Fiction. 2. Manned space flight--Fiction. 3. Extravehicular activity (Manned space flight)--Fiction. 4. United States. National Aeronautics and Space Administration--Fiction.] I. Roski, Gayle Garner, ill. II. United States. National Aeronautics and Space Administration. III. Title.
   PZ7.O46828End 2013
   [Fic]--dc23
                                                        2012040567

ISBN-13: 978-0-9856237-2-2 Hardcover
Printed in China
Published in the United States of America

Quiz Answers: 1.a 2.b 3.d 4.c 5.b 6.a 7.c 8.a 9.a 10.d

GLOSSARY

air lock: a device that allows astronauts to go from inside of a spacecraft to outer space

flight deck: part of the space shuttle where astronauts fly the space shuttle

galaxy: a group of billions of stars

gravity: force of attraction between all objects in the universe

International Space Station (ISS): facility in space where astronauts from 16 countries conduct science and research in space

Magellanic Clouds: galaxies neighboring our Milky Way galaxy that are visible from Earth

meteorite: a natural object originating in outer space which sometimes survive impact with the Earth's surface

mid-deck: part of the space shuttle where astronauts eat, sleep and conduct research

Milky Way: galaxy that contains our planet Earth and our Solar System

mission: task or project

orbit: path followed by an object in space, such as a satellite or moon, as it travels around a larger object

payload bay: the "trunk" of the space shuttle where astronauts can spacewalk to build and fix spacecraft

satellite: object that travels in a circle around another object, such as the Moon traveling around Earth

shuttle: a reusable spacecraft to take and return items from space

spacewalk: the activity of astronauts using a special white space suit to work outside of the spacecraft.